A
POWER
FAMILIES
ADVENTURE

To Lilu, POWER ON! - S.M.
For Tori x - A.E.

Russell DeLeon, Executive Producer
With Special Thanks To Our Renewable Energy Champions:
Turner Foundation, Inc.
Stephen Cordova

Jack Hook Publishing
1288 Columbus Ave, #279
San Francisco, CA 94133

First U.S. Edition: 2011
Library of Congress Control Number: 2011933265
ISBN: 978-0-9837863-0-6

10 9 8 7 6 5 4 3 2 1
Printed in the United States of America.

Flo & Mo Power
and the
Big Storm

A POWER FAMILIES Adventure

Story by
SUSE MOORE

Illustrated by
ANDY ELKERTON

Jack hook

Out on the deep blue ocean Mo was jumping waves.

His sister, Flo, popped up next to him with Socket at her side.

"Come on, Mo, we've got to go. Mom's got a surprise for us," she said.

They raced through the wave energy fields back to the Power House.

A mysterious object sat bobbing on the water next to the jetty. "Surprise!" said Mom.

SWISH! She pulled off the cover.

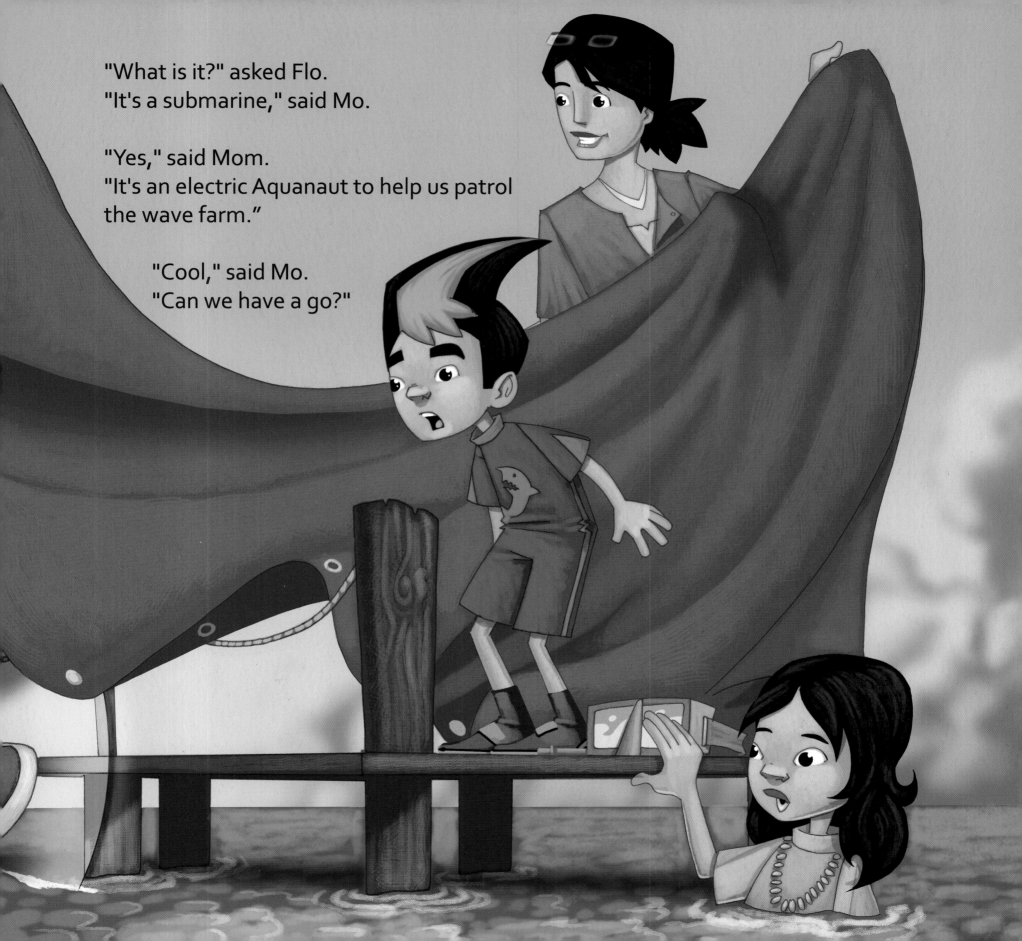

"What is it?" asked Flo.
"It's a submarine," said Mo.

"Yes," said Mom.
"It's an electric Aquanaut to help us patrol the wave farm."

"Cool," said Mo.
"Can we have a go?"

Mom touched the control panel.
The screen lit up and the
Aquanaut's engine began to hum.

"Can I drive, please?" asked Mo.

"All in good time," said Mom, closing the hatch.
"Now hold on tight!"

She pushed the steering wheel forward.
The Aquanaut dived under the water.

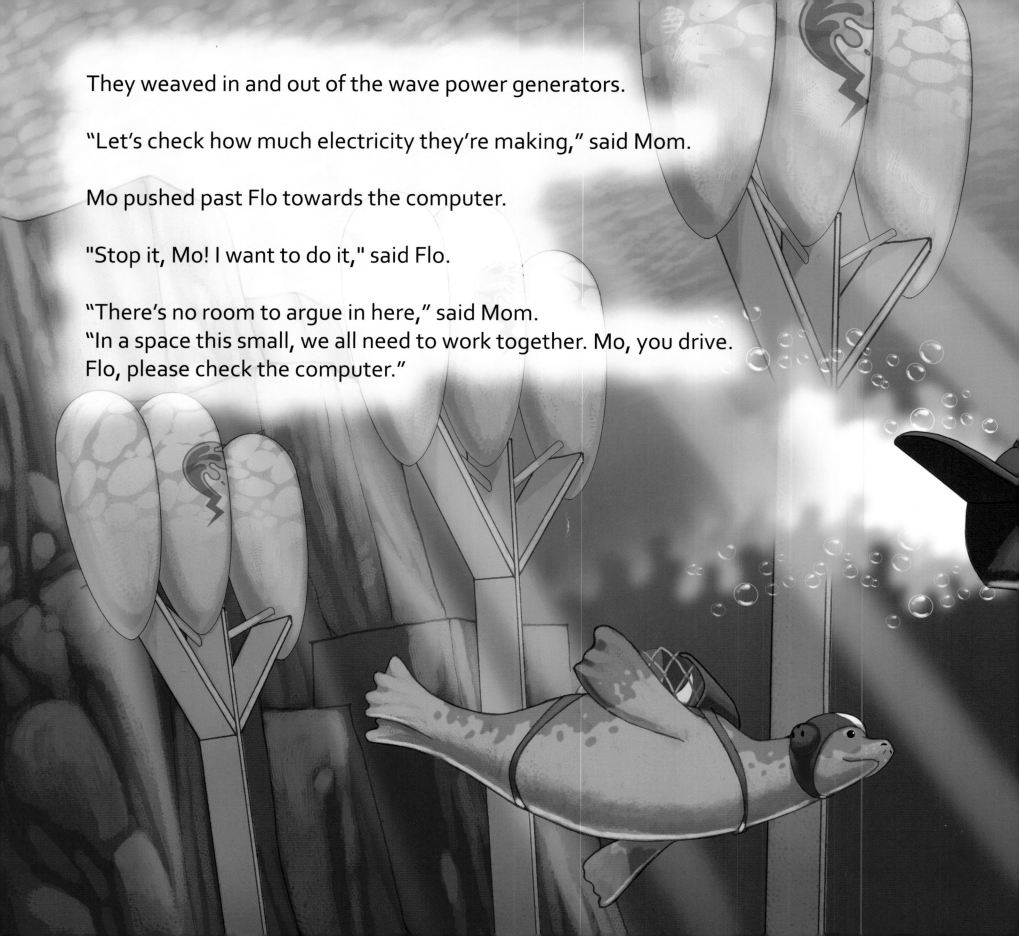

They weaved in and out of the wave power generators.

"Let's check how much electricity they're making," said Mom.

Mo pushed past Flo towards the computer.

"Stop it, Mo! I want to do it," said Flo.

"There's no room to argue in here," said Mom.
"In a space this small, we all need to work together. Mo, you drive.
Flo, please check the computer."

The Aquanaut burst out of the water.
The hatch slid open and Flo jumped out onto the jetty.

"That was amazing!" she said.
"I think you've both got the hang of it," said Mom.
"But next time drive slower, Mo. Socket had to race like a rocket to keep up."

RUMBLE! RUMBLE! thunder boomed in the distance.
"That storm is coming in quickly," said Mom.

"Let's recharge the Aquanaut and hurry inside."

Flo and Mo both reached for the cable.

"Go ahead," said Flo.
"No, you do it," said Mo.
"Let's do it together," said Flo.
They plugged it in as the rain started
to fall.

Outside, tall waves crashed over the jetty.
Lightning crackled across
the night sky.

Mo was under the sheets reading a scary book.

RUMBLE

"That was some storm," said Mo, the next morning.

"Look!" cried Flo, pointing at the computer screen.
"The sonar's picked something up."

A black shape loomed large in the center of the screen.

"It's the monster! It's found us!" cried Mo.
Flo giggled. "You're so silly, Mo."

Mom frowned. "That shape is something big and it's heading straight into our wave energy fields. It could damage the wave power generators."

Flo jumped to attention.
"Mo and I will check it out in the Aquanaut right away."

"All right. I will stay here and make sure it doesn't cut our electricity supply to town," said Mom. "Please be careful."

Flo navigated using the sonar
as Mo slowly piloted the Aquanaut.

"We're never going to get there," grumbled Flo.
"Speed up!"

"No. We must go slowly," said Mo,
thinking about the monster in his book.

"Stop!" said Flo.

Mo slowed the engine.
Above them bobbed a big,
rusty sea container.

"That's not a monster," said Flo, laughing.
"It must have fallen off a ship during the storm."

"I was only joking. I was trying to scare you," said Mo, boldly.

He piloted the Aquanaut up closer to the container.

Two long, metal claws
snaked out of the Aquanaut.

Flo guided them carefully
towards the container.

CLUNK!

"Got it!" she said.

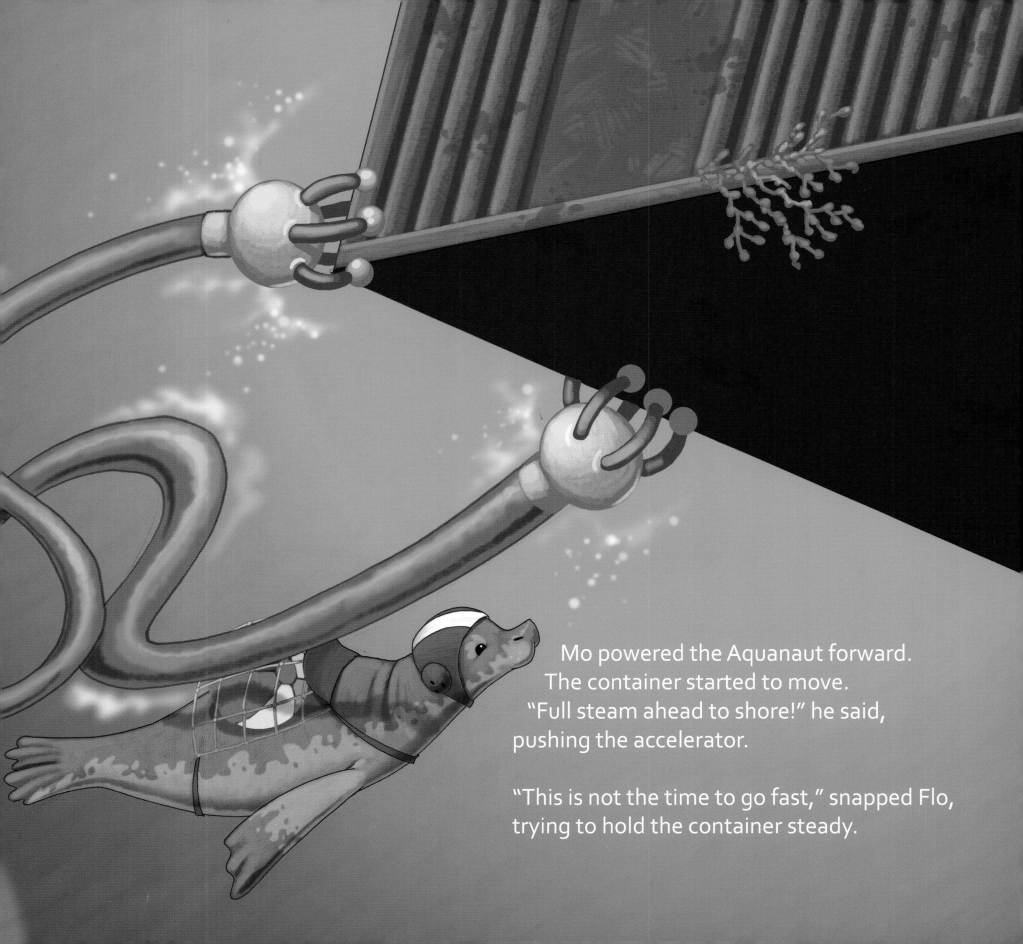

Mo powered the Aquanaut forward.
The container started to move.
"Full steam ahead to shore!" he said,
pushing the accelerator.

"This is not the time to go fast," snapped Flo,
trying to hold the container steady.

Mo raced the Aquanaut up to the surface, nearly crashing into the jetty.

"Stop!" cried Flo.

Just in time she lifted the claws, landing the container with a thud next to Mom.

"That was close," said Mom. "What teamwork!"

"I'm going to see what's inside," said Mo, leaping onto the jetty.

Before anyone could stop him, Mo released the container door.
Thousands of toy ducks came tumbling out on top of him.

"What an interesting gift from the big storm," said Mom.

"Quack!" said Mo, covered in ducks.
"Quack!" laughed Flo. "I know just what to do with these…"

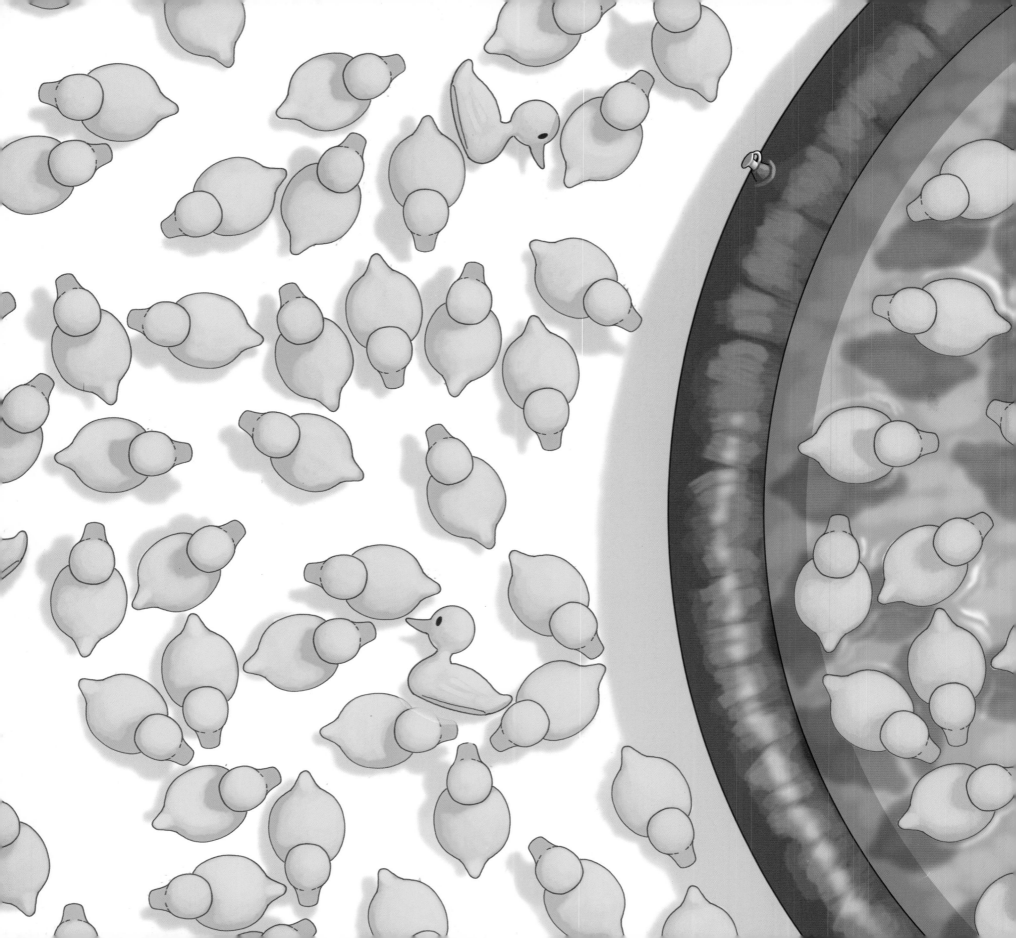

THE END